Chris Fite-Wassilak is a writer and curator based in London. He frequently contributes to Art Monthly, Tate Etc., and other journals. His essays and articles elaborate on art, cultural histories and moments that break open to the uncertainties of chance.

Ha-Ha Crystal is titleset in re-drawn cut of Clarendon by Ray Larabie. It is typeset in Lido Condensed, a typeface originally commissioned for the Czech newspaper *Lidové noviny (People's Newspaper)*, designed by František Štorm.

GW00758865

COPY PRESS

*What day
of the
month is
it?*

Chris Fite-Wassilak

HA-HA
CRYSTAL

CHRIS FITE-WASSILAK

The Copy Press Limited
51 South Street
Ventnor
Isle of Wight
PO38 1NG

copypress.co.uk

Commune no. 10
Editor Vit Hopley
Reader: Yve Lomax
Copy-editor: Sara Peacock
Design: Ivor Williams

Front cover © Chris Fite-Wassilak

Printed on Munken Print White
no.18 80gsm. Munken Print White
standard products are FSCTM
and PEFC certified.

Printed and bound in England.

First edition © Copy Press Ltd/
Chris Fite-Wassilak, 2016

Chris Fite-Wassilak asserts the moral
right to be identified as the author of
this work.

A catalogue record for this book is
available from the British Library

ISBN-13   978-1-909570-03-0

The philosopher no longer laughs, must not laugh.
Laughter is not an 'argument'.
Denis Hollier, *Against Architecture*

HA

The forest had been laid flat. A few electrical utility poles stemmed up from the rows of shattered stumps of pines. I had emerged from a grey shaded incline that had let me only hear the light English rain as I'd walked up, arriving onto the fell and a recognisable walking path. Following the path around a corner, sticking out on its own was a slim, sick-looking heart of a tree, the lone survivor of whatever raid had taken place. I tried to match the lines etched in the clearing around me to the simplified, rounded abstractions on the map of the park I'd just been given. This starved totem seemed to roughly match one of the dots. Underwhelmed but oriented, I walked on.

There were a few particular points on the map I was intent on finding, so I started by heading towards one. Descending back into a forested area, I came across a sculpture standing next to the path, a squat lion-like figure in stone, its corners and crevices blackened with mould. This, as far as I could tell from the map, was meant to come further along after what I had been looking for. I walked back up the hill a few metres, in from the path to the other side of a small furrow. Behind the brush amongst the leaves and low ferns was a pile of even, thin rotted poles of wood, greening with moss. I gathered that this, looking like long-discarded firewood, was all that was left of an artwork placed there decades earlier.

This experience repeated itself throughout the sculpture park; the numbers dotting the map were slightly off or missing altogether. Finding them, or their remnants, was more accident than anything else. Straying off one path led to a small clearing where a ramp of concrete rose up unexpectedly out of the ground. Two young trees shaded it from view, aided by the grass and ferns sprouting freely from the structure. Stones half-hidden under a layer of damp leaves, unusual bumps on the ground or fallen branches tangled in the bushes became subjects of close attention. Any unattended pile of wood became a potential collapsed artwork, lost to the elements and the bureaucracies of time. Walking the forest paths in the hills of Cumbria that autumn after-noon felt like I was shadowing the sculpture park. Misplaced co-ordinates led me to its parallel, a place where outdoor sculpture had been disowned and left to rot. This feeling was punctured only occasionally when encountering a passing trekker; I wondered if we were even walking on the same paths. Eventually, doubling back on myself on another failed route, I had mused enough on the discrepancies to stop and examine the map in more detail. In small print at the bottom was the date 1997 – I'd been treading some version of these paths from fourteen years earlier.

During the summer when I was a kid, my or my friends' parents would sometimes take us to an amusement park just outside of the city. It was an hour's drive, far enough away for the trip to feel like a big deal, though the fuss might have also been more the result of the adults dragging their heels and rolling their eyes, having regretted ever giving in to our repeated demands. Six Flags Over Georgia's main attraction was the rollercoasters, the oldest being a fairly sedate up-and-down-a-few-steep-hills affair and the newest, at that time, a compact vertical stack of tight turns that had a zippy, zero-gravity-invoking title and came shrouded with rumours that children had died falling off. Both petrified me. We would spend the day harnessed into plastic seats, gripping the bars tightly as we zigzagged backwards and forwards in the air. At the ride's peak, ticking slow inches towards the verge, we glanced across the flat lay of the Georgia landscape, at its low, square roofs grouted with the green of pines. Maybe we would've noticed two reddish angular poles sticking up above a nearby road, just across the slow, brown trickle of the Chattahoochee River that runs behind the park, and maybe we wondered what they were.

Small motorised trains ferried us from the vast parking lot to the entrance of the amusement park and back to our car at the end of the day. We were not aware that these same trains had been used at the development just across the river twenty years earlier, carrying guests at an opening event from one concrete platform to another concrete platform, each at the time mounted with a different sculpture. Once we set off in the car for home, heading back east on the cracked tarmac of

Atlanta's highways, resting our whiplashed little heads, we didn't stop. Had we made the detour a few minutes down the road, we would have seen a two-hundred-foot-wide framework made up of tubular steel poles long ago painted red, the entrance to Six Flags Over Georgia's intended twin, the Great Southwest Industrial Parkway.

Texan property magnate Angus Wynne Junior, CEO of Great Southwest Corporation, had set up a successful Six Flags in his home state. He had a plan: build another amusement park to bring in the crowds and provide the adrenaline rush, while simultaneously opening an open-air museum, a place where those same crowds could be cultured. He hired a range of high-profile specialists to carry out his plan, and commissioned over forty out-door sculptures by a handful of American artists who had come to prominence in the 1960s. An art historian later said that the Great Southwest Parkway was, at the time it opened in 1968, the 'largest public collection of monumental contemporary sculpture in the world'. Dorothy Dehner, the artist who designed a Plexiglas relief for one of the brick walls in the parkway, had high ideals for the site: 'Instead of an industrial slum growing just anywhere, deteriorating even as it is born, the Industrial Park is conceived as a center of industry in terms of reason and beauty. It becomes a place to be admired rather than an unsightly complex to be avoided.' By the time I was born in 1981 the area had become exactly what she had so enthusiastically promised it wouldn't be. Some twenty sculptures remained, a few unattributed, many rusting and peeling – 'a cemetery', the art historian eulogised, 'of late 60s Minimalism'.

Corporate suburbia is a desert that reclaims any untended land. The parkway collection, at first a Who's Who of minimalist sculptors of the time, quickly became indistinguishable from its setting. Many of the artworks that were present at the site, such as Dehner's relief, disappeared. Some were scrapped, some were sold to a local art dealer ending up in a series of property developments; a few were donated to an art museum several states north by the insurance company that took over the Parkway three years after it opened. Others apparently found new homes; a few are dotted around the dusty libraries and county offices in Atlanta. One, a small angular cross resting on its side, sits outside a government service centre north of the city; the title of the work and the artist who made it are no longer known, an anonymous tribute to its lost history. Now, you would have to know that the area was once a sculpture park to even find the scant, arid traces of what was once there; only the hollow, angular red archway remains.

The red archway – a structure named the 'Atlanta Gateway' by its maker, Peter Forakis – is an uncomfortable, leering herald, vaulting over a turn off the oversized lanes of the highway that it faces. Three long poles, two on one side of the double lane leading into the Parkway and one on the other, angle up. Over-lapping in the middle, they stretch up to meet crossbars that complete the outline of two sideways pyramids balanced over the road. It is both precarious and imposing, appearing as a massive line drawing that swivels, then solidifying and falling apart again as you drive towards and under it. This provides the entrance to what otherwise seems like any other part of sedate, suburban Atlanta: faceless single-storey buildings, each set amongst the pool of their own empty parking lots, a place without pedestrians, without any sensible atmosphere, the kerbside grass a thinning brown with bald patches. The occasional empty concrete platform doesn't look too out of place amongst the storm drains and service access points that dot the roads; only the marks of cut bolts and rusted screws allude to something that might have rested on top in the dry, blank sun.

Forakis's two giant, see-through pyramids are still one of the largest pieces of modern sculpture on the planet. It's apt that they look over this no-man's land like a decaying monument of a civilisation, an echo of the Mayan or Egyptian pyramids. Their shape also resonates with other, more modern markers that aren't as aspiringly eternal: things like geodesic domed greenhouses nestled in humdrum botanical gardens, filled with green, sweating misplaced micro-climates, or the giant glittering golf ball of Disneyworld's Epcot Centre.

Led by the hand up into the underbelly entrance of the spherical centrepiece of the Epcot Centre, my five-year-old self would not have known why it was called Spaceship Earth. I would have just thought it was a cool name for a giant silver ball. Its surface was pocked with a pattern of bulging triangles; inside, pre-recorded voices guided us towards clunky passenger carts that they described as time machines; the ride glided us slowly past panoramic displays of telephone exchanges and oversized computers. Only years later would I hear the phrase 'Spaceship Earth' again and understand it more as an idea to turn the imagination of an age obsessed with space travel back onto the planet itself. Presenting himself as systems manager for how humanity might guide itself out of the mess of the mid-twentieth century, it was Buckminster Fuller, an idealistic and ecologically minded businessman, who popularised the term. His *Operating Manual for Spaceship Earth* proselytised a highly engineered but light-impact future; Fuller imagined a new architecture starting with the pyramid. Conjunctures and manipulations of the shape formed the basis for his designs, including, most famously, his patent of the geodesic dome – the Epcot golf ball was based on Fuller's designs. In the Atlanta Gateway, the kissing pyramid tips have just met, perhaps on their way to crossing further, inter-penetrating and interlocking to form what Buckminster Fuller called a 'duo-tet'. The resulting star-shaped structure would be angular and resilient, the building block for an architecture of tomorrow. But the Gateway only suggests that union, remaining on a threshold over the abandoned plinths.

In a dense and prismatic essay by stone enthusiast Robert Smithson, the pyramid surfaces again, cast as a 'chuckle' in a categorisation that pairs types of laughter with crystal structures. This unlikely alignment is claimed as a method to visualise the fourth dimension. 'Entropy and the New Monuments' describes the art being made by a dozen or so artists whose style was gradually becoming known as Minimalism; Smithson conjures up the boring, shiny lobbies of office and apartment blocks that were popping up all over the place in the late '60s as the appropriate setting for this new type of sculpture. But he does this skittishly, roping in on the way countless passing references to science-fiction films, thermodynamics and psychotherapy. The short text spills over with alluring contradictions and snappy inconsequentialities, like: 'Time becomes a place minus motion.' The artists and artworks he discusses take second place to his staccato rhythm and the distracted web of his imagination.

The closing paragraphs remain the most enigmatic, perhaps for their suggestion of a potential tool: the ha-ha crystal. Smithson starts the passage with an abrupt claim: '[Buckminster] Fuller was told by certain scientists that the fourth dimension was "ha-ha," in other words, that it is laughter.'

He moves on without stopping to explain: 'Laughter is in a sense of kind of entropic "verbalization." How could artists translate this verbal entropy, that is "ha-ha," into "solid-models"?'

The first time reading these sentences, I was struck by how casually it tossed aside any apparent hurdles – tying together the desire for projective thinking from science, architecture, literature and art – towards a vision of the fourth dimension that was already there, already rising up in our throats as laughter before we even knew how to speak. But then he didn't seem to find such laughter in the straight-edged minimal artists he was talking about, but almost despite them, beyond them. The question of how 'ha-ha' might be translated remains open. Not to leave us entirely hanging, Smithson jumps to provide one answer in the form of his idiosyncratic taxonomy of laughter, matching each with a geological crystal structure:

the ordinary laugh is cubic or square (Isometric),
the chuckle is a triangle or pyramid (Tetragonal),
the giggle is a hexagon or rhomboid (Hexagonal),
the titter is prismatic (Orthorhombic),
the snicker is oblique (Monoclinic),
the guffaw is asymmetric (Triclinic).

The 'ha-ha-crystal concept', as Smithson called it, is entertaining and at least obliquely insightful and perhaps indirectly useful – or usefully indirect. According to his taxonomy, the Atlanta Gateway becomes an amplified double chuckle, echoing over the tarmac – a chuckle, a half-committed laugh, a light-handed admission of amusement; it's perfunctory, used when someone has said something that is supposed to be funny, but you didn't really get the joke – given the history of the Great Southwest Parkway, it might sound a little sardonic. And Buckminster Fuller's architecture takes on the sense of almost accidental accumulations and overlapping chuckles – the enclosure of a geodesic dome turns into a seething riot of misheard quips and misunderstood humour. Yet Robert Smithson's concept asks for other responses, other surfaces that might contain and elicit further reflections. The potency of the ha-ha-crystal concept hovers around its multiplicity, in its ability to gather an unlikely and improbable nexus of ideas together and act as a meeting point and gateway between them.

The laughter continues to echo unbidden.

> I do what I can, alas!
> To be wise,
> To exercise my freedom;
> But if some young beauty,

Borrowing your vivacity,
Spoke to me in your lovely language,
I would soon return to captivity.

The literary gazette *Mercure de France* was rife with
such roundabout flattery and emotional declarations
throughout 1732. Here, the writer who called himself
Voltaire teases that he might be drawn out of his self-
imposed life of celibacy by the verses of the mysterious
Antoinette Malcrais de la Vigne, an unseen author
who had become known in French poetry circles as *la
muse bretonne*. The editor of the *Mercure* was slightly
more forthright, inserting in one edition the note, 'I love
you, fair Breton; forgive me this avowal, but the word
has escaped me.' The poetess and her poems had captured their literary imaginations and quickened their
studious hearts.

Their public proclamations, however, had the effect
of prompting the Madame Malcrais to reveal that she
was actually a man. The poet, a rural accountant, was
quickly discarded by his former admirers as a hick with
more ambition than talent. Voltaire, attempting to save
face, continued to stay in touch with the aspiring poet,
offering advice on both his verse and useful connections.
Not long after, in what turned out to be their last letter,
Voltaire recommended that he kept his day job.

Voltaire's numerous critics preferred that the
incident not be glossed over so easily. *Metromania* by

Alexis Piron premiered in Paris in January 1738, a comedy written entirely in rhyming couplets, about a male law student and would-be poet who publishes under the pseudonym Madame de L'Empirée. This tale of ghost-written love letters and mistaken literary ambitions would be Piron's most popular work, and the most lasting tribute to what was by then widely acknowledged as the distinctly forgettable poetry of Madame Malcrais. Piron's protagonist is described in the opening of the play as an absent-minded type who gets so absorbed in his creative work that he forgets the world around him: *S'approchant pas à pas, d'un ha-ha qui l'attend: Et qu'il n'appercevra qu'en s'y précipitant.* (Approaching step by step a ha-ha that awaits him: and he won't see what he's rushing into.)

When compiling his dictionary of the French language, Émile Littré saw fit to include 'ha-ha', defining it firstly as an offhand insult for an older woman of unbecoming appearances, and then as 'an obstacle suddenly interrupting a path' or 'an opening made in a garden wall with a ditch on its outside to leave a free view'. The first edition of the Littré from 1863 includes the quote from *Metromania* as an example of usage for the second meanings.

A ha-ha, these days, is still a landscape design feature: a ditch in a park or garden that separates different levels of manicured lawn while giving the appearance of the higher land flowing seamlessly into the grounds

below and beyond. The moment of the 'ha' that supposedly provides the feature with its name has been given
a range of explanations: for some it's the cry of delight
at the unimpeded view; for others, it's the sound of
surprise made by walkers finding that their path is
blocked by a ditch; others again have pinned it as the
taunting laugh of lords and landowners watching
ignorant peasants fall into the gap.

The ha-ha originated in early eighteenth-century
French pleasure gardens, though in the years that
followed the practice took off in England's parks and
stately homes more so than France. The feature's hidden
ditch helped shape the broad vistas of the designs of
influential gardeners like Capability Brown, allowing
the sense of unending nature while managing to keep
unwanteds, animal or otherwise, at bay. Later editions
of *Metromania* use the word *fossé* (ditch) in the
place of 'ha-ha', but the original script was one of
the earlier recorded uses of the term. The commonly
cited first recorded mention of the 'ha-ha' is in *The
Theory and Practice of Gardening*, a 1709 hand
book by French royal secretary and garden connoisseur
Dezallier d'Argenville. The passage hidden in his lengthy
manual, though, actually describes something else:

> Grills of iron are very necessary ornaments
> in the lines of walks, to extend the view, and
> to shew the country to advantage. At

present we frequently make thorough views, called *Ah, Ah*, which are openings in the walls, without grills, to the very level of the walks, with a large and deep ditch at the foot of them, lined on both sides to sustain the earth, and prevent getting over; which surprises the eye upon coming near it, and makes one cry, *Ah! Ah!* from whence it takes its name.

At some point the surprise turned to laughter: D'Argenville's 'ah-ah' is the same as Littré's 'ha-ha', a sudden break in a garden wall. The laughter eventually became a disappearing trick: both the ah-ah and the ha-ha make use of a ditch to create an unimpeded view of the surrounding countryside – but what has come to be known as a ha-ha does so by sinking the garden wall into the ground.

It doesn't stop there, of course. In a recent academic paper, British literature professor Derek Connon claimed that Piron invented the term 'ha-ha'. It was conjured by the playwright, he said, to describe an already existing gardening design, used just once, at the play's very beginning. *Metromania* might well be the first appearance of 'ha-ha' rather than 'ah-ah' – Connon's referenced source, however, is a Littré dictionary printed the same year as the premiere of Piron's play. Littré was not even born at this point – he didn't start writing his tome until over a century later.

The play, at the very least, does prove to be a locus where the chatter and pitch of this laughter reverberates that bit louder, that bit more rapidly. You can imagine Piron revelling in the befuddlements, giving gleeful outlet to the impulses of his metromaniac with the endless rhyming possibilities between the mirrored ah and ha.

With the confused origins of the ha-ha, Robert Smithson's jump to conclude that the 'ha-ha' supposedly whispered into Buckminster Fuller's ear was laughter starts to seem a bit hasty. The 'certain scientists' that Smithson breezily attached his conviction to might well have meant something else altogether – that it was an architectural ha-ha, an image that suggests the fourth dimension as a kind of hidden ditch, a gap in our perception with the illusion of continuity; or, that the fourth dimension was just, after all, a joke.

In all the back and forth, it could well have been the inverted, original 'ah-ah' that they meant: an utterance that, instead of the breakdown of language, suggests a moment of surprise and an interruption of space. The 'ah-ah' turns Smithson's concept into a breach in perception and a means of conceiving of a strategic collapse of space: through the interruption we can see the vista of the fourth dimension.

If I then combine the ah and the ha, the ha-ha concept is modified to create an 'ah-ha crystal'.

The palindrome made of the two becomes an act of sculptural summoning, an 'ah' raising the wall from the ground and a 'ha' lowering it back down again. The ah-ha crystal becomes an imaginary pivot around which to consider these gaps, jumps and invisible ditches.

What Robert Smithson, Buckminster Fuller and his gaggle of scientists have in common is a desire to articulate something just beyond our grasp. Between Piron's and Smithson's 'ha-ha' is the suggestion that ideas like 'time' and 'space' are not only inextricably linked but intimately felt, things that are embodied and handled casually in our distracted and skipping minds. The ah-ha crystal is an imaginary tool they unintentionally inspired; what it suggests is that these overlapping, overlooked and hidden layers are always there, accessible through certain gateways.

HA - HA

AH

AH

A H – A H

A rasping exhaled breath with words barely carried out on it, weakly coasting along for the ride. The words thick and sandpapered, you lean in to aid their delivery. The weighted effort is felt with every grating, rumbling attempt at release.

I've never lost my voice. I've had thick coughs where the sound has come out squat and rasping, a swamp voice where I found a perverse pleasure in how different it was from the usual tones that came out of my mouth. I've been elbowed in the stomach and winded for a few long minutes, lying there rocking back and forth and mouthing like a goldfish while my insides sucked at me like a dry plunger, surrounded by air that I un-believably wasn't allowed to let in until the thick heaving finally let off. When friends had laryngitis and couldn't speak, I was thick-skinned about it. The exaggerated miming gave everything they did a theatrical tint, as if they'd made up their illness.

Hanging out at the neighbourhood pool when I was a kid often meant holding our breaths underwater for as long as possible. I'd learned to dribble out a bit of air, let my body sink to the bottom and settle like debris in the pool's deep end while the timer on my digital watch reeled forward. When it became clear that an attempt wouldn't be breaking that day's record, we'd expend our remaining air trying to speak: opening our mouths, bubbles tripped upwards with every word. Regardless of how loud or clearly we tried to speak, our words became a series of murmuring honks or low, flatulent wails. My breath would run out so quickly, but in those seconds I felt as close as I could be to sound. It was as near to my ears as it was my feet or the top of my head, enveloping me for that moment before I had to finally push back up to the surface.

Years later, as teenagers in school, we would go through the charade of being a Model United Nations. Each of us would be assigned a country with the understanding that we were meant to represent that landmass and its population, ostensibly speaking for their concerns and future plans in an ordered debate. You would raise a placard with your country's name on it to either question the country who had the floor or to take the podium yourself – Resolution 254, on the banana embargo; Resolution 587, on the border dispute between Cambodia and Laos – each mediated by rules of procedure, points of information, amendments to certain wordings and eventual voting. It was a miniature mockup of a global system within which we played at being grown-ups. It's easy to see why the model was created: it taught restrained argument, it gave an idea of how 'real' politics might be acting at the same time, as well as being a fairly overt indoctrination of the ideals of the UN itself. We'd do this on a small scale with twenty of us in the school gym every few months, and then once a year on a larger scale with thousands descending for a week on The Hague.

Dress a teenager up in formal office wear and you might get them to aspire to a better vocabulary, but the arena of the Model UN inevitably provided a space for the micro-politics of school drama to repeat themselves. As we pretended to take on the concerns of our respective populace and go through the motions of a debate, those who were loud-mouthed, confident and outspoken filled the meetings with rhetorical flourishes and endless exceptions; those given to introversion and quiet generally remained so. I went along to the monthly Model United Nations meetings for over four years, but I think I got up to speak in front of people at most twice. I was into the idea of an international forum; I also thought I understood what it was to be the voice of a nation. But I was also mortally shy, getting fidgety and nervous as soon as I planned to say something out loud in front of a large group. So I said nothing. I convinced my-self instead that it was pointless, that these mock meetings were the opposite of debate, and the endless deferrals just the complicated passing of hot air. Most travelled to the event in The Hague for the excuse to hang out with the other boys and girls from all over the world who were there for the week. During the time we were there, we probably reflected the adult version, in endless meeting rooms and bars, more accurately than we even knew.

One friend, a tireless socialiser and eager debater, was so enthusiastically involved in the activities both in and out of the plenary sessions that after two days she couldn't speak any more. She spent the rest of the week scribbling notes and gesturing wildly.

'Having a voice' is a phrase generally reserved for political terrains. It's used to urge people to take part in petitions, protests – to speak out. In halls and meeting rooms, debate rules are designed to ensure that speakers have their say, or at last are given a chance to try. Outdoors, overturned shipping boxes and crates become an immediate platform to shout from in parks and on street corners. While governance may reside largely in the written forms of laws, letters, applications and affidavits, and carried out through the physical actions of the police and the military, these activities are thought of according to the spoken word. Having a voice, speaking out, being heard or silenced: the mechanisms of politics are shaped by the metaphors of speech and sound.

'Your vote. Gotta have it!' An advertisement shouts from a wall in the Hong Kong subway system. The slogan was part of a campaign by the government, initiated by the announcement that the former colonial territory would have its first popular elections. The posters were placed all over the city, their tone a meeting of the civic and the commercial as if pitching democratic activity like

34

a collectable toy. The summer of 2014, pro-democracy groups staged small gatherings; some of the younger attendants in the crowd waved Union Jacks. In August, the mainland Chinese government announced their proviso that they would pre-approve the candidates. By the end of the year, the tear gas had dissipated, and the police and insistent volunteers were clearing away the last of the cable-tied barriers and ribbons of tents that had made up the protest sites where thousands, mainly students, had blocked some of the city's main thoroughfares for weeks. The adverts, with their urge 'Let's seize the opportunity to achieve universal suffrage', were gone by then and the precise scope of what they meant had become clearer – everyone *could* vote regardless of *who* they were allowed to vote for.

The campaign's main graphic was a simple outline of a rounded rectangle with a small triangular bit protruding from the bottom: a speech bubble. In one version of the advertisement, a red arrow on a black marble floor points towards a polling station; in another, a white ballot box sits locked on a glass table. In each, a speech bubble is superimposed on the image to look as if it is the arrow and the ballot box that are saying the 'Gotta have it!' tag line. During the protests, the Hong Kong pro-democracy movement set upon using a yellow umbrella as their symbol, but the bubble – an ideal tool for their struggle – had already been implicitly tied to it.

The speech bubble is graphic shorthand for saying something, anything. It's brandished across bus-stop advertisements; it shapes text messages on our phones. It can carry sentences, single words, punctuation marks, pictograms or nothing at all. The bubble is the means through which figures, drawn onto and bound into the printed page, can speak. It's a blank space where sound is converted into concise text – recalling those half-conscious moments when we began to link what we hear with what we read.

The ways into language are slow and sideways, re-gurgitating and tethering half-swollen noises, latching them onto passing shapes and floating notions. Sounds get tied to words, a set of letters in which the sound is held latently, to be woken upon reading. These tethers for sound are impressed onto paper, folded into news-papers, bound into books, lassoed into balloons. Language spreads: I grew up surrounded by animated, jabbering cats, mice, sponges and paperclips, never really questioning how they were speaking in the first place. It turns out it's the talking animals that led the way in the birth and developments of the speech bubble over the past century.

The languid and impatient caterpillar in Disney's animated interpretation of Lewis Carroll's stories of *Alice's Adventures in Wonderland* smokes a hookah, dispelling fumes as he sings, 'A–E–I–O–U...', each letter, perfectly formed in smoke, emerging from his mouth as he makes its sound. Spotting Alice perched listening at the base of his mushroom divan, he stops singing to ask her roundedly, 'Who are you?' An 'O' billows forward, shot through by a small, pink 'R', a wispy 'U' curling underneath as the letters travel from his puckered lips towards the curious girl. He appears nonchalant about his talents in what might be described as a form of visual onomatopoeia.

Tintin's white terrier Snowy (or *Milou*) began his life a talkative and opinionated animal. In their travels to Russia in 1930, the dog spoke two hundred and thirty times (usually about how hungry he was). Throughout the stories, their speech bubbles spring from their mouths with small lightning bolts, each a miniature transmission. By the time of Tintin's last adventure in the fictional South American dictatorship of San Theodoros almost fifty years later, Snowy pipes up only once. The gradual and consistent decline of Snowy's chatter might be due to the increased realism in the style of drawing, which brought with it the implication that animals shouldn't be speaking. Or perhaps Snowy was no longer needed as a character foil, as Tintin himself and his other – human – companions became more fully developed. My own suspicions, though, are more sympathetic with the dog: Tintin never acknowledges any of the dog's commentary – four decades of being ignored might gradually silence any of us.

But it was to be a small green parrot, an animal already known for being a talker, that signalled a shift in how we hear voices on the page.

Like the faces in cameos
I wanted beloved voices
To be a treasure one keeps forever.

The poem laments a dream, or rather its displacement from its author, the poet Charles Cros. He had submitted designs to the Academy of Sciences in Paris for a cylinder, which could record and replay 'acoustic phenomena', but his bohemian lifestyle didn't provide him with the means to ever make the machine. His vision was not unfulfilled; the voices he described were instead collected by someone else. Eight months after his submission, a wealthy, well-connected and half-deaf inventor was publically conducting his own tests on such a device. It was Thomas Edison, despite decades of other competing attempts to make visible and capture sound, who would proclaim himself the inventor of the phonograph. The machine was envisioned as a tool for recording the voice, capturing it as something that could then literally be had, owned and stored. Edison presented a jumble of tubes, wires and cones in the 1889 Paris Universal Exhibition, with twenty-five different versions of the machine playing phrases spoken in over a dozen different languages.

On the trip to Paris, one of Edison's employees from his lab in New Jersey, Richard Outcault, was brought over to document the display. He had been Edison Laboratories' official draftsman for a year, though he supplemented his work with the occasional cartoon sent in to the humour magazines. Outcault's cartoons were often bustling scenes of tenement houses, crowded celebrations of roughed-up children of immigrants living in urban squalor. When the four-colour rotary press allowed for a Sunday colour comics supplement to the broadsheets, Outcault created the Yellow Kid, a scrawny, sickly looking bald boy wearing a stained, loose-fitting yellow gown who gormlessly wandered New York's alleyways. The Kid's own misspelled enunciations were scrawled on his gown like a sandwich board.

'Listen'te de woids of widom wot de phonograff will give yer', the Kid's gown read one late October Sunday, seven years after Paris. The Kid proceeds to have a conversation with the 'phonograff' in front of him. 'Why is de Sunday Journal's coloured supplement de greatest ting on earth? Say!!! Dat's too easy,' the horn of the phonograph announces, 'It's a rainbow of colour, a dream of beauty, a wild bust of lafter'an regular hot stuff.' In the last scene, a panel at the base of the machine opens, a parrot walks out and looks defiantly up at the Kid with a small speech bubble emitting from its mouth: 'I am sick of that stuffy little box.' The surprise also seems to have knocked the Kid sideways enough that his words migrated from his gown to his own floating speech bubble.

Outcault's cartoon is often misattributed as the first use of the speech bubble as an active voice on the page. He was certainly well positioned to make a connection between his employer's machine and how speech was could be represented visually. Other cartoons and comic strips from the time, though, had also arrived at the same solution, some even featuring parrots and telephones to get the idea across

Bubble-like shapes had been hanging around for a while. Earlier, they had been read as static reports and descriptors, not as speech events or pictures of sound. Unravelling scrolls that provided names and incidental information featured in paintings from the middle ages. Olmec and other Mesoamerican cultures had begun using symbols to depict speech thousands of years earlier, most often in the form of question-mark-shaped lines, or at times snakes or daggers, curling out from figures' mouths. Political cartoons of the late seventeenth century were filled with labels, billowing and bulbous containers where characters were speaking, though not to each other. These bubbles were understood as the author's intervention, each bubble a description of someone's role in the puzzle that the reader was trying to decipher. It wasn't until the invention of the phonograph that the notion of a captured 'sound picture' separate from the body became imaginatively possible –

and that the illustrated figures on a page might be understood as speaking for themselves over a duration with responses, reactions and consequences.

Edison claimed to have made speech 'immortal'; the process of capturing it had transformed its corporeality. Speech written on pages for centuries – in dialogues, quotes or the yammering of characters in stories – had been static, transfixed. But there was something that was, as it were, in the air, a shift that made the page sound different. The speech bubble became an enunciation from within the page, legible as a series of speech acts in the present; a present that could now be sequestered and replayed on a whim.

The word for the speech bubble in other languages is telling: in French *bulle* also means a lacuna, a gap; in Italian, a *fumetto* is a little puff of smoke. I see the bubble as an unstable object, uncertain whether it is a hole punched out of the world of the story or a whited-out space. I can see it and can't see whatever's behind it; for the characters within the page, I assume it's the opposite. Sometimes its intrusive enclosure is nudged at, acknowledged, but it doesn't pop or disperse. The bubble hovers on the edge of dimensions and media, a valve from within the two-dimensional world that translates sound to text, and inflates it with a contradictory physicality. I don't quite trust it: somewhere there is a leap of faith that I'm 'hearing' correctly – that what I've read is actually what had been said and is attributed to the right person, or that everything uttered is there. I keep wondering about what happens to all the other incidental, accidental, ignored sounds, about all the other noise

In what came to be called 'silent' film, most talking was represented with caricatured expressions and wild gesturing. As film lengths grew, intertitles became a more common method of cutting in plot explanations and quotations from the characters – the floating words were left shuddering on screen just long enough for the audience to read. In Japan, live narrators, the 'katsuben', were positioned next to the screen, providing descriptions of the plot as well as speaking for all the actors. A resident of Winthrop, Massachusetts, Charles F. Pidgin, sought to avoid all such interruptions to the flow of the story. Pidgin made a living from his literary creation Quincy Adam Sawyer, detective and dashing young man for whom 'strange adventures and unexpected experiences were the breath of life'. Aside from his novels, Pidgin was also an engineer and inventor who submitted numerous patents for tabulating machines. One successful patent from 1917 was for a 'motion picture and method of producing the same'. In his application, he describes the actors within a film each having an inflatable device which would have their words written on either side. The coiled up device when blown by the actor would unfurl so letting the audience know quickly and easily who said what. For Pidgin, the 'blowing or inflation of the devices by the various characters of a photo-play will add to the realism of the picture by the words appearing to come from the mouth of the players'.

Pidgin supplemented his patent application with a set of diagrams that illustrate the use of his device. Two oblong balloons bob above lovers sitting on a beach. 'I never loved her' reads the one floating sideways above the man, the shape casting a shadow on the rock they lean against. 'You did once', hers reads. Underneath is a portrait of a man with Pidgin's inflatable device unfurled in his mouth, reading 'How nice of you'. It seems comedic now to think of the speech bubble being lifted from comics and transposed as an inflatable balloon to film. And it must have seemed equally ridiculous to producers of the era: Pidgin's idea never got used.

In just a few years, several other methods had been established for coordinated sound and image projection. Pidgin found success at the very least as an inspiration; his patent was referenced as a basis for several later patent applications. One from 1950 described imposing speech bubbles on photographs as a method for making instructional films; another from 1994 was submitted by the company Readspeak, Inc., who sought to replace subtitling in films with their own made-up term of 'euthetic (well-placed) captioning'. Single words would be placed next to the actor's mouth as they were heard, following them around the screen as they moved.

The dream that all of these tinkerers and inventors share is to capture the voice, to hold onto it as a way of documenting and experiencing the world more completely, to coil the line of the voice around itself and shape it into an object that can be moved and released again in another place or a later time. A linguistic miracle – Edison's later trademarked gramophones each bore a small illustration of a young angel holding an oversized quill, inscribing around themself a circle of record grooves. What this new technology also made apparent was that the voice could retain its sense of immediacy, and at the same time be disembodied and replaceable. Cylinders and coils of words could be handed from one person to the next to be unwound. The medium that carried the speech itself became more potent than any speaker.

The story of the bubble is the search for its tail. The tail of the speech bubble points to who is meant to be uttering the words. It doesn't, however, tell us who is actually speaking, but rather who, or what, is allowing us to access speech in this way. It points to another listener that precedes us, harvesting sound inside the page. Someone or something has placed the bubble there and chosen what sounds have become closed off and legible in this manner. The familiarity of the speech bubble hides what its predecessors – the labels and scrolls lurking around paintings – openly acknowledged: the bubble is put there by the narrator or whatever shadowy entity that presides between the author and their creations.

It is this ambiguous authority that gives the speech bubble its potency, the ability to make anything appear as if it is speaking. Placed over any image, it can force figures to emit words that they never said. Celebrities in gossip magazines might expound complex economic theories. Politicians and models in advertisements might shout out racist jibes. Or ballot boxes might make disingenuous claims for democracy. This is its attraction and also its insight: the modern, liberated speech bubble silently points towards the outlines of – and constraints on – speaking and hearing. The bubble carries with it an implicit demand that we recognise who is being permitted to speak and the barriers and bodies that it moves between. Speech is always framed, permitted, delivered. Its tail points towards authority; and while we constantly assume different voices, we also speak in the place of others and silence those sounds that might seem incidental. This authority is still fluid and layered – the act of enunciation is shaped in an instant, and can be reclaimed or relinquished in just as long. We often divest ourselves of these politics and locate them outside of ourselves, when their continual closing-offs are already all around us, enveloping us, tripping out of our mouths.

HA

AH

The house was struck by lightning when I was four. It hit a lower part of the roof, cutting into what was then my bedroom. The incident has been retold to me so many times since that I have no idea how much of the scene I've imagined or not. I was apparently standing in the doorway; there was a still darkness tinted orange by the traffic outside. I remember a loud crack. A ball of bristling white light travelled around the square room, spinning its way twice around the ceiling before disappearing. A red after-trail faded more slowly. There remained a black spot in the corner, as if that was where the lightning had just stabbed in and left again milliseconds later. The heads of the nails in the walls were bare, stripped by the electricity.

The way I think back on it now is not so much that I was lucky to be unhurt but more touched, awed. It wasn't merely an encounter with atmospheric insta-bility and an electrical storm; I was a privileged witness to an apparition. What are the chances – I was made to think by countless cartoons, films and murmured urban myths – of getting hit by lightning? A once-in-a-lifetime occurrence. Lightning is the ultimate idea of an event, each time unique and impossibly quick.

The unbridled energy of the lightning bolt makes it the ready bearer for a broad range of symbols – the cartoonist or filmmaker's go-to sign for ominous things to come, the graphic shorthand for danger or speed. Lightning is an analogy for thoughts, ideas or inspiration,

49

a jolt of energy and illumination, instantaneous and gone just as quickly. We position ourselves like metal rods, seeking the conditions where we might be struck; a place, quiet, solitary, maybe high up on a hill, where thinking can be done, where notions might arrive in bursts, sparks and flashes.

Everything was made up of air, some ancient Greece thinkers claimed – our thoughts were merely a less condensed form of the element. In one satirical play, *The Clouds* by Aristophanes, the philosopher Socrates is introduced sitting in a basket hung from a tree, claiming that he has to 'suspend my brain and mingle the subtle essence of my mind with this air, which is of the like nature, in order clearly to penetrate the things of heaven'. The protagonist of the play is a scheming old man who comes to The Thinkery – or in some translations The Thoughtery – a stable for training philosophers-in-the-making, to learn the art of rhetoric in order to be able to evade his impatient creditors. Socrates, head of The Thinkery, boasts in the play of such intellectual achievements as deducing that a gnat's arsehole must be trumpet-shaped to produce the sound of the insect's buzz and developing a measuring tool based on a flea's leap. He begins his lessons by pointing the old man towards some clouds in the sky, describing them as goddesses who, in their suggestible shape-shifting, provide the inspiration for all 'thoughts, speeches, trickery, roguery, boasting, lies, sagacity'.

Aristophanes' play ends with the old man beaten and kicked out of his own house by his son. His response to this and his oddball lessons is to take a torch to The Thinkery and burn it down. Socrates, busy postulating inside, suffocates on the fumes. The thinking of the historical figure of Socrates is known only indirectly through the writings of his students and other writers from the time; the play, although a satire, was cited by Socrates' student Plato as one of the reasons Athenian public opinion turned against him. Socrates was tried for sacrilege and carried out his own execution order by drinking hemlock.

The conception of thought as air continues to drift up through to the seventeenth century. Descartes took more than a passing interest in the growing anatomical sciences and saw our thoughts as originating from airborne animal spirits, spirits he described as a 'light wind' that flowed from pockets at the base of the brain throughout the body. Ideas and imagination were a result of the impressions that these spirits made on the pineal gland, a small, cone-shaped organ at the centre of the brain. Like a miniature cinema, ideas would be traced on the surface of the gland, and memories were formed from the afterglow of those tracings.

The pineal gland's singular position at the top

of the spinal chord and between the two hemispheres of the brain was what made it appear like an important organ. For Descartes, the gland was the bridge between the mechanical body and the mind that controlled it. This gland, a flickering cone, was what enabled us to interact with the outside world. It was the physical basis for our immaterial selves, the throne where our soul sat.

These days, we understand the pineal gland regulates our sleep through the release of melatonin; the spirits are now electrical impulses that travel along the nerves. But Descartes's tiny cone cinema isn't as far fetched as it might sound, given what can now be pried from inside a skull. The flickering images of the mind have become Technicolor: magnetised scans of the brain show patches of pulsing bright blue, green, yellow and red – watch the brain at work, parts of it glowing like an ember. The attempt to find a precise location in the brain for where the mind resides has fragmented into areas like the right parietal lobe, the temporal lobe and the prefrontal cortex. Researchers have developed software to read the electromagnetic signals that our brain emits – one study asked people to read speeches by Abraham Lincoln or the nursery rhyme Humpty Dumpty; the recorded signals were then run through a computer model of the brain. A coherent reconstruction of the phrases came out almost two-thirds of the time, in a slightly muffled, gargling voice: 'a new nation conceived in liberty and dedicated to...'. A related study asked people to watch clips from Hollywood film trailers. The moving images they managed to salvage from the minds of participants are scratchy and blurred with vague outlines and rough colours; faces appear more distinctly, while text is a dissected set of dense, hatched lines. The studies refer to words in the subjects' heads as 'covert speech'– as if, in the minds of the researchers, the words we might be about to speak and the thoughts in formation are simply hidden objects, like maybe a stone or a wayward sock, waiting to be uncovered and revealed. The phrase 'you read my mind' becomes quite a literal prospect. The inside of the brain is no longer a black box but an erratic filter, a hazy transmitter that we have only to learn how to tune.

Having a thought is one thing; keeping it, finishing it, giving it a full stop – when we get the thinking, as it were, done – is another matter entirely. Any half- or fully formed thought, if we could ever call it that, faces the task of articulation, the translation to another, external, state. How thought is portrayed isn't, of course, the same as thinking, but perhaps it can reflect the efforts of that translation. We use streams of consciousness, flights of fancy, trains of thought – things in motion – to speak of processes of the mind. I can try to note down an idea as it occurred moments before, then stare down into the yawning gap between the words on the page and the things in my head that have already shuffled helplessly onwards. And sometimes, too, there is a chiming of some form of accord between them, but it's a neat trick of fiction to think that we could ever think of thought as something fully knowable or comprehensible; as if a proportion of firing neurons might have a well-rounded, grammatically immaculate sentence ready to be delivered. The acceptance of hearing and reading thought as such is what I find fascinating. The voice-over in film or a literary aside make thought seem accessible and fulfils other urges – itching to know what others are thinking, fancying our own articulations to be so groomed, so astute. Another of these fictional methods floating nearby, the comic book thought-cloud, is a telling weathervane for thinking about thought.

The thought-cloud was an innovation that followed on from speech bubbles, developed alongside 'talkie' films as a transformative narrative invention of the early twentieth century, though a quieter, more insidious presence. Like the speech bubble, it provides text in a whited-out space that hangs around the heads of characters. It's as if the speech has evaporated, with smaller puffs that lead from the thinker to a larger pillowy shape with softened, billowing edges. In its haze, private musings and passing fancies are extracted and given a textual presence on the page. The thought-cloud cradles thought, like Socrates in *The Clouds* when, still hanging from a tree, he describes 'these baskets, in which we suspend our minds'. It's a neuroscientist, psychologist and philosopher of mind's fantasy: direct, legible access to an inner world.

Where the sound picture of the speech bubble asks for one form of belief – that what is read was what was actually said – the thought-cloud asks for another entirely. Its visibility and seeming independence, afloat out there on its own, sets it apart from other representations of thought. I like, perhaps as any reader, to think that fictional characters get up to things out of sight, that they roam as they please within their own worlds, that they are more than an arrangement of lines and words. Fairly or not, we expect at least some prying into their heads, some access to their emotions, thoughts and hidden workings. The thought-cloud, though, is an intrusion of the highest level, and an extrusion: within the thought-cloud, private, scattered firings are bundled and arranged into words, phrases and sentences that can be understood outside of the character – from their mind but separate from it. What this presents is not just the representation of thought as language, or language as a synonym for thought, but the equation of the two. It's a one-to-one relationship between internal and external states – the word is the thought, and vice versa.

It's a fictional convention but a risky one, following through with the idiom of reading someone's mind. The act of reading these words presupposes an inextricable link between what is written and what is meant. The mind is treated as consisting entirely of covert speech that can then be taken out and coherently read, and that the inscription and the essence are in true accord.

> Hence it happens that sometimes a man is called a pig on account of his sordid and piggish life; a horse, on account of his endurance, for which he is remarkable above all else; a cow, because he is never tired of eating and drinking, and his stomach knows no moderation. (Paracelsus)

The names of animals were, according to the sixteenth-century Swiss occultist and alchemist Philippus Bombastus von Hohenheim, indications of their true qualities, and could as such be applied to any human who shared those attributes. Hohenheim, who had renamed himself Paracelsus, believed in a 'science of signatures' as a means of reading the true nature of things from external signs. Visual resemblances of plants to certain parts of the body were indications that they could be used as medicinal herbs for ailments of that corresponding area. Bodily deformities were signs of internal vices. Considering himself a practitioner of the signatory art, locating these signs in the weather, the stars and on the body – and, crucially, finding the right words to describe them – was a means, he thought, to both understand inner essences, and to control them.

Taught by Benedictine monks, Paracelsus had derived his relationship to words from the scriptures. Divine utterances were, by definition, true; what he saw in the Old Testament was the first example of humans also being able to practise an utterance that is at the same time its essence. After the mythical first human being, Adam, is formed from earth, the Old Testament describes all the world's newly created animals being paraded one by one before him. Adam assigned each of them a name, and whatever he called each living creature, well then that was its name – a deer was a deer, a hummingbird was a hummingbird, a platypus a platypus and so forth. Adam was the first to use the signatory art, as he accurately named everything on the earth according to their qualities, with names that were, Paracelsus insists, 'ratified and confirmed by God'.

Names and words were the keys to this art – external, readable portals to the mind. What the thought-cloud proposes is a widespread return to the science of signatures, where an acute incursion into a character might be made from reading the words hanging over their shoulders. The danger of the signatory art, like any principle based on judgements of outward appearances, is that it depends on who is doing the reading. For Paracelsus, any aspiring practitioner must understand the natural, astral and celestial signs before attempting the signatory art; it is to be approached with utmost caution by a select few. The thought-cloud, instead, makes it look like a casual dispensation, a rampant outpouring of words as consciousness.

As the winds continue to blow, the thought-cloud's projection of the mind as readable and portable pre-cipitates other formations. The Cloud is similarly a small airy fluff that follows us around everywhere, where we can store things like some kind of omnipotent hand-basket; a pervasive, ever-present parallel dimension we can all access anywhere, at any time – as long as we have a wi-fi connection. The Cloud holds a mind that can be saved and swapped, that animates the mechanical body of the phone, tablet or whatever device we happen to be using.

Cloud computing doesn't just rely on the same imagery as the thought-cloud, it also shares its relation-ship to the word. Online search engines are driven by the attempt to know what's being looked for, providing arranged results according to what a set of algorithms think we want to find. Predictive text models on phones second-guess what's being typed before even one letter has been entered. Internet search and purchase histories are used to tailor personalised advertisements; typed-out names of places and objects mentioned in messages are taken as indicators of our hobbies and interests. Music collections, lists of phone numbers and endless emails are stored in an immaterial, unlocatable else-where, all represented by the simplified outline of a single cumulus cloud. The transient, floating imagery hovers in direct contrast to The Cloud's very physical basis in a rooted set of wireless internet ports, subterranean cabling and anonymous-looking data storage centres around the world.

Under the shadow of The Cloud, thought is a conglomeration of typings and transactions, read and cross-referenced by non-human eyes. The logic of The Cloud breezes over Paracelsus's wariness to automatically generate a list of personal attributes and concerns. Words become a set of categorised 'key-words'; desires become 'recommendations for you'; these accumulatively become The Cloud's portrait that it attempts to project back as an accurate reflection. Implicit in Paracelsus's instructions of the signatory art is the acknowledgement that outward narrations can interfere with the unknowns of the human interior – how we think about thought mingles and messes with how we 'hear' ourselves think. In The Cloud, we can't hear ourselves think any more because its version of our mind is already there, cached, ready to be downloaded.

Even by the time Descartes was postulating about a fiery air coursing through the veins, the body that he imagined had already been overtaken by new ana-tomical discoveries. His theories of the pineal gland never caught on. Centuries later, however, the pineal gland would again be conceived of as a central part of the human mind, but this time of a distinctly more feral nature. It was, according to the archivist and philosopher of excess Georges Bataille, the place where an uncontrollable unconscious raged, a fervent energy opposed to all of the logic and science that has come to dominate society. In his essay 'The Jesuve', Bataille described the gland as 'a sexual organ of unheard-of sensitivity, which would have vibrated, making me let out atrocious screams, the screams of a magnificent but stinking ejaculation'.

The pineal gland is an evolutionary vestige of the parietal eye, a light-sensitive opening near the top of the skull found in some reptiles and fish; it's also known as the spiritual third eye, an opening that connects us to the skies. For Bataille, the pineal gland was a potent spiritual seed of our animal ancestry, a connection within us with the scents and scurries of the ground that we lost when we began to walk upright. The gland was the outlet for the unthinking urges that had been forgotten, overlooked and subsumed: 'Men spit, sough, yawn, belch, blow their noses, sneeze and cry much more than the other animals,' Bataille wrote, 'but above all they have acquired the strange quality of sobbing and bursting into laughter.' It was these necessary, unexplainable emissions – of chortles, smut and bile – that Bataille thought were the most honest and revelatory: we might dress and order our deliberations in fine words, but our thoughts shouldn't be, can't be, comprehensible.

The thought-cloud, like both Descartes's and Bataille's pineal gland, makes visible the invisible in an attempt to understand and translate the workings of inner experience. It represents an impossible dream that has turned in on itself, as it quietly facilitates an illusion that thought is actually finite and knowable. What thought can be becomes precise and affixed, in a radical simplification of inner life; the thought-cloud, as one imaging of what we might imagine thought to be, leads instead to a distorted, static mirror.

We will, as ever, continue to prospect and recast the contours of the mind. Aspects of the brain, I hope, might always remain covert; the project to comprehend the mind could, like Bataille, be deliberately stalled, or abandoned altogether. The thought-cloud remains a notion that can be reshaped and set towards more wayward ends. We can still envision other lives of the cloud. Its space can also hold other visions, other ways to begin thinking of thought; perhaps as something incoherent, abrupt and unfinished, that erupts and dis-appears again like lightning.

AH

HAYSL*

A H – H A

C R Y S T A L

You get out of the elevator, stepping from its glass floor onto the springy fuzz of the green and gold carpet. You walk over to the balcony, lean over it, and run your eyes over the repeated lines of the other floors arrayed before you.

After a long while, having seen no one else around, you go into your room. The view is underwhelming – the block of apartments opposite just reflects back the patterned lights of your own half-empty hotel.

The building straightens and stretches.

Here, you might imagine the block of apartments as a page.

You might then bend and fold the page.

You could roll it into a cone, layering and spiralling the apartments in a compacted curve. You could, chuckling to yourself, fold it once diagonally downwards to make a triangular overlap, the building's upper rooms now facing into the middle floor.

Or you could fold the entire page twice, down in thirds upon itself to form the façade of the building into a triangular prism, and, guffawing louder now, peer into the now adjoining rooms reflecting off each other like a kaleidoscope, the inhabitants gesturing to each other through the angled windows from different times. Here, in the crystalline comic city, is a vision of a possible ah-ha crystal.

Overlaying the prism of the folded building-page, everything around you takes on another shape

A H – H A

– misrecognised, alien, shockingly and pleasingly so. Looking through the prism, you view an endless, replicating orthorhombic network of identical doorways. You open one, to walk through and find stretching out before you a levelled forest, your laughter echoing amongst the thin, shattered stumps of pines.

CRYSTAL

The author thanks the Hospitalfield Ken Cargill Writer's Fellowship 2015, for the invaluable time to write, and the residency at Hong Kong Baptist University AVA in 2014, where the initial steps towards this book were taken. And thanks to Ger O'Donoghue, Orit Gat, Paul Becker, Dennis McNulty and Lilah Fowler.

VIT HOPLEY
Wednesday Afternoon

Wednesday Afternoon is a collection of prose that introduces awkward perspectives on all manner of things: a house taken on an arduous journey across a frozen lake, a puff of dust released from yesterday's socks, a death in a basement, a gathering of strangers. Vit Hopley pays attention to every detail. She writes on sitting, standing and lying down, but most significantly she creates a stillness that is almost photographic.

'Wednesday Afternoon *has shown words anew. It's very much like fresh rain and fresh air.*'

PHILIPPA BREWSTER

MICHAEL SCHWAB
Paris

Michael Schwab is curious about trees in Paris. The most unnatural thing about a tree in a city is the place where it is planted. A tree in a city does not grow; it is planted. *Paris* lets you explore trees in Paris while it breaches narrow definitions of photography.

'So you think you know Paris, but if you take Michael Schwab as your guide you will find yourself in a truly inventive space between photography and drawing. You will be delightfully transported to spaces and places of the imagination, with some very particular trees to hold on to for reality. This is indeed Paris from another perspective.'

VANESSA JACKSON

JASPAR JOSEPH-LESTER
Revisiting the Bonaventure Hotel

This book is a photo-essay that describes the life of a building through a range of film stills, photographic images and written citations. With *Revisiting the Bonaventure Hotel* we wander between references to Fredric Jameson, John Portman and Arnold Schwarzenegger as we view a world through different perspectives: vertical, horizontal and rotating. This is a story about the image.

'I loved it. Looks like a Chris Marker book, so glamorous.'

CHRIS KRAUS

HAYLEY NEWMAN
Common

Through fact and fiction, questions and answers, writings from the heart and writing from the street, *Common* chronicles one day of a Self-Appointed Artist-in-Residence in the City of London. Performances occur and reoccur as this book takes us to crashes in global markets, turbulence in the Euro-zone, riots on hot summer nights and the most extraordinary imaginings.

'The financial sector in the City of London is often viewed as an impermeable, inaccessible block, and that perception is what gives it a lot of its power. In Common, *Hayley Newman has subverted that, opening the City up through richly imaginative stories that are at once creative examples of how to play with the space, and empowering political actions. I hope this book will inspire others to embark on similar transformative adventures.'*

BRETT SCOTT

ANNE TALLENTIRE
Object of a Life

Oscillating between depiction and description, *Object of a Life* addresses the question: How are we to speak of common things? Making an inventory of things that come to hand in the course of daily life, playing with ideas of contradiction, categorisation, improbability and speculation, this book offers an articulation of the space produced between language and drawing.

'*In* Object of a Life *Anne Tallentire extends her enquiry past the objects of everyday life to ruminate on the space in between and around the objects' relationship to their sites of activity including the domestic, the studio and the street. Like all good artists' writing, this book calls upon us to think differently...*'

LISA PANTING

JAKI IRVINE
Days of Surrender

In 1916, when Padraic Pearse, Irish republican and leader of the 'Easter Rising', decided to surrender, he asked midwife Elizabeth O'Farrell to make the perilous walk to deliver his message to the British army. Setting off down a Dublin street where some of the dead still held white flags in their hands, Elizabeth O'Farrell was watched from the door by Julia Grenan, referred to in documents as her 'friend and lifelong companion.' This is the story of those days.

C O N T E N T S

HA

DIAGRAMS FOR SERIALITY
Neil Chapman

Diagrams for Seriality is a book of unforgettable images and strange characters. Here the reader is thrown into a world where expectations of series and sequence are turned inside out; this story creates a narrative of haunting and mysterious affect.

'*A startling meditation on the relation of seeing to saying, the possibility and impossibility of communication, and the very business of making and writing* – Diagrams for Seriality *is a work of fictioning in which set pieces and scenes, a cast of bodies and conceptual personae and a singular prose style produce a book that demands to be reread.*'

SIMON O'SULLIVAN

FALLING
Kreider + O'Leary

This book begins in zero gravity and ends with everything flowers. In between, figures are falling as we hear something about philosophy, laughter, architecture and war. With writing and drawing coursing through its pages, *Falling* gathers momentum and, through this, a picture emerges: it looks something like today.

'Falling *is a work of natural philosophy, about wire-walkers and moonwalkers, elevators, angels, slapstick, skyscrapers, swerves, and the dynamic figure that links them. Here Kreider + O'Leary describe 'the beautiful mess we're in' with a speculative precision. Their description of falling, in its uncoupling of the tyranny of cause and effect, displaces the now-prevalent despondency of end-thinking with a prolific joyousness.*'

LISA ROBERTSON

ILSE AICHINGER
The Bound Man

The Bound Man is storytelling for our times. Here we find works of fiction where a present darkness and obscurity usher extraordinary performances into the light of day: a man bound hand and foot; a death told in reverse; a speech under the gallows. Written with disarming simplicity, this collection of stories puts language to the test.

I remember reading The Bound Man *many years ago. The story has never left me. Reading it now, along with the other stories, I am again caught in what feels like the confusion of shock, where time is fluid and the material world is an uncertain, unstable place, full of fragile hope and loss. I experience the shifts and startling turns in these stories, and their imagery, as unexpected blows to the heart.*

JAYNE PARKER

HA

A H – H A

A large outcrop of granite sits just east of Atlanta, though all you will see from the top is the compact cluster of skyscrapers not far off in the city's centre. Atlanta is pretty much flat – as a child, when thin layers of snow fell the most I could do was roll a short distance down a brief incline. Reaching any altitude was a novelty. I remember going twenty-two stories up to a blue dome that topped a downtown hotel; next door was an even taller hotel, cylindrical, clad with glass and a rotating cocktail lounge at the top. I went up there once as a treat when my grandparents came to town. We sat at a thin glass table, staring out the window while I sucked at a foamy kid's version of a piña colada with a paper umbrella and one of those translucent coloured plastic sabres sticking into a radiating maraschino cherry. Outside the whole state slowly turned by as we wondered at the view and tried to trace the long roads to locate where we lived, played, went to school.

I grew up believing that all cities were like Atlanta: a small, concentrated centre of sleek, vacuous buildings that stood guard over unused sidewalks, surrounded by a front-and-back-garden suburban expanse where the majority of life happened. City centres weren't places to be visited in themselves but rather where you might make brief incursions for events in convention halls and stadiums, or the occasional trip to the museum. Stumbling in to other cities with jostling, sprawling centres was a revelation; though Atlanta's peculiar tone has spread. Large sections of its centre were designed by one person, architect John Portman. I hadn't realised his reach until I'd travelled to Los Angeles for the first time a few years ago and found that, despite its hyper-mythologised sprawl, chunks of its downtown looked and felt much the same as Atlanta. His hotels look like huge apartment blocks, but turn their bulk into a conference centre retreat. Portman found a formula for profit by embodying the combined role of both developer and architect for his projects, turning large stretches of inner city blocks into oases for people to attend meetings and go about their business lives without ever having to step outside. Atlanta was his first testing ground, and sizable chunks of Detroit, Los Angeles, Shanghai and Beijing have since followed, carrying the same overbearing manner. It appears that he neither added to nor fixed the centres he built in, but rather ignored them, as if trying to replace them.

The innovation commonly attributed to Portman is his use of tall, sweeping atriums – perhaps it was the evenness of Atlanta, his adopted hometown, instilling in him a desire for vistas and elevated sightlines. The hotel topped with the blue dome was his first project to feature a high, enclosed atrium, with brightly lit pod-shaped glass elevators running the full height of the building. These expansive indoor spaces became his signature; they were repeated in his template buildings and copied throughout the world – you still hear architecture students that claim Portman invented the atrium.

The atriums of his I've been in have been identically impressive and overwhelming. Balconies stack up above you, the rooms set like an impossibly tall beehive; you feel small and absorbed into a wider order. Taking the glass elevator up, you see each floor going past with the same doors, the same carpets, the same layout. The sense of innumerable lives being lived simultaneously in identical rooms accumulates. Although you might not be able to see more than one or two floors at a time, the architecture suggests that with the right perspective you will be able to take in all the floors at once. It's a self-justifying design: you can see all the floors so you can ... see all the floors. Or, perhaps more accurately, you have the illusion of having access to every floor, making the entire building available to your imagination. Portman's buildings are other- wise remarkably blank, with the distinct feeling walking around inside – no matter how many people around you – of being empty and abandoned. They are designed for legions of lone out-of-town businessman, who survey the expanses of the brightly lit atrium and the city outside at a safe distance.

A father flicks on a television, his bald head illuminated by its glow as he settles into a stiff chair for the evening. He is in one of a half-dozen apartments with full floor-to-ceiling picture windows, their tastefully decorated interiors visible from the street. The apartments are arranged in a small grid over two floors, each kitted out with a vase of flowers, some nondescript art on the walls and a couple of the black leather chairs. The families in the other apartments are also gathered in their adjacent sitting rooms around flickering televisions. The television sets are all embedded in the thin walls that separate each apartment so – from where we're watching them – when the families are looking towards their televisions it looks like they're staring directly at one another. It's as if they can also see through the walls – one family appears to balk at their neighbour's drinking habits; the bald man begins undressing while the woman next door fidgets nervously as if in response.

In an empty lot on the outskirts of Paris, Jacques Tati built his own compact vision of a modern city from scratch. The apartments frame one scene in his film *Playtime*, which takes place in a city that appears to built almost entirely from glass, a labyrinth of endless shiny surfaces. His film set was inspired by the new business districts going up in cities across Europe at the time, filled with a grid of identical glass box structures. A fleet of miniature office blocks on wheels served as moveable backdrops to make sure that any view in the film would always be squared off and hemmed in by a seemingly endless row of pristine buildings. In Tati's city, the families' confusion and crossed sightlines are a regular occurrence.

Architects of the late nineteenth and into the twentieth century envisioned glass structures as a liberation that could transform spaces, to let in light and open them to the world. *Playtime* poses a tongue-in-cheek what-if premise, reimagining Paris as almost entirely see-through. Tati, a long and lanky music-hall performer who had made his name doing pantomime impressions of rowers and rugby players, played Monsieur Hulot in each of his films – a mumbling, scurrying everyman attempting to come to terms with new technologies and modernity's wacky new materials, usually with slapstick disastrous results. In *Playtime*, he's let loose in a crystal maze of near-identical offices, supermarkets, cafes and sitting rooms. The plot, if it can be called that, is simply that Hulot tries to make it to an appointment and fails, thwarted by the architecture itself. Every interior we see feels the equivalent of a cor-porate waiting lounge, quietly controlled, all sleekly minimal in blacks and silvers, mirroring itself indefinitely. Different rooms and visible planes become confused and squashed together, become accidentally and randomly merged, sliding and shifting with every step.

When Hulot is ushered by an old acquaintance in to one of the picture window apartments, Tati demon-strates what transparent living produces: the ability to look at people in buildings. The lives of the families in the apartments are on full view for any passer-by to gawp at. Why not, Tati suggests with the inter-apartment charade, treat the walls between dwellings as see-through, too? The apartment scene sits as the film's epicentre, with the tacit acknowledgement that the transparency of the modern city in not just the letting-in of light but also the letting-out of life; that visibility goes both ways, or even multiple directions at once. 'Tativille', as the temporary city-set that bankrupted him came to be known, proved to be unexpectedly pre-dictive of the architectural landscape to come. The apartment scene, though, wasn't included in the film's original release: it was only incorporated for the first time in a new edit fifteen years later, a few months before the director's death.

Almost a century earlier, in a darkened theatre, a young woman sits among the audience looking towards a stage. The play being acted out on the stage is a production of Shakespeare's *Hamlet*: it has reached the third act, when the royal court has itself been turned into a stage for a performance of a short murder mystery Hamlet has called 'The Mouse-Trap'. The prince, excited and agitated, sits on the floor, not watching this play within the play, but looking at his royal audience to gauge their reactions. The young woman, similarly, isn't watching the court performers; she is staring only at the actor playing Hamlet. Looking at him looking – with a vague awareness that other things are going around him, that the play is running on without her paying attention – she feels uneasy, but not uneasy enough to stop focusing exclusively on the seated prince. She only wonders about the growing disparity between what she is feeling and what is happening on the stage

Years later, she described the experience as a sensation of nervousness, in a lecture titled 'Plays'. Visiting the United States from Paris for the first time in thirty years, the author Gertrude Stein toured the country performing in cities or universities one of six prepared lectures delivered in her quick and looping voice. In this lecture, Stein spoke about watching *Hamlet* in language that was both precise and elusive:

> Your sensation as one in the audience in relation to the play played before you your sensation I say your emotion concerning the play is always either behind or ahead of the play at which you are looking and to which you are listening.

There is an directness to Stein's words; her repetitions begin to feel as if she was using words like objects, shaking and rattling and trying to wear them down to see if they could get tired, sputter out; or, to see if something else might spring out from the agitation. There is also in her tone, and throughout her work, the stance that I have come to recognise as someone who had left the United States and was dissecting it with the tender and curious ambivalence that only leaving provides.

Americans were, in Stein's view, best positioned to see the coming twentieth century; there was enough of a hastily wiped slate and a freshly concocted culture to be able to embrace the undefined 'newness' of the age. In her writing and lectures, Stein is far from a nervous character; yet part of the disposition she sought to cultivate was not just comfort with, but a celebration too, of unease and displacement. It was this unease she found as 'the thing that is fundamental about plays', how the linear running of a play becomes complemented and co-opted by other trajectories. This productive unsettling was a feeling she also found, as she goes on in the 'Plays' lecture, in the bumps and edges of a music that had begun to form as she was growing up, and that would eventually be labelled jazz. 'They made of this thing an end in itself' – the 'thing' being a shifting, disjointed attempt to describe her awareness of this sensation of nervousness, a feeling that she seems hesitant to fully pin down. 'They made of this different tempo a something that was nothing but a difference in tempo between anybody and everybody including all those doing it and all those hearing and seeing it.

Stein presents that evening watching *Hamlet* as her earliest memory of when she felt time bifurcate, an experience she names as theatre's syncopated time. Syncopation describes the accenting or displacement of musical rhythms, or the unpronounced parts of words that are present only in spelling; as Stein proposes it, the word also describes a layering of contrasting attentions, understandings and desires, how the distances between bodies might be crossed. Sitting there, watching or listening, isn't just letting something happen to you, it is an uneven negotiation on invisible terrain.

Seeing can be thought of as a form of narration and a kind of ownership. The theatre's invisible fourth wall lets us look in, survey the characters and listen in on their goings-on for a few hours. From her seat in the audience, Stein could have dwelt on any of the critical moments in realising the play – in, say, the relay between the Shakespeare and his choices in writing the script, between the script and each production bringing it to life, or between the slight variations, changing emphases and mistakes in every performance. But she instead thrummed on the overlaps of perspectives and the skipping threads of attention. There's a charge to the way she appreciates how to look, and how to be seen – her nervousness discloses an unease with any singular narration, an unease with authority.

Stein's circling around this 'thing' highlights the back and forth of connected but disjointed realms that might overlay, intertwine and blur between the sensory and imaginary, reality or fiction. Syncopation is a tangle of rhythms that quickly spirals outwards, away from the stage and off the page; it's a nervousness that might be sensed in any number of places. A layering of divergent attentions, desires and emotions is persistent but unpredictable, in albums replayed years after being recorded, an old book casually picked up again, or in the remnants of a misplaced, anonymous sculpture; the relays span milliseconds and millennia. I enjoy how from a lecture from the 1930s, repeated to different audiences a only a handful of times, comes the suggestion that just being in the world can be acknowledged as unstable, as a sort of time travel.

I relish her elusiveness; a nervousness that is both personal and shared, that can't be defined but only conjured, gestured towards; it – if this 'thing', this something that is nothing, can be called an it – is, as Stein put it, a thing to get by getting.

Jump forward from Stein's lectures thirty years to Tativille's gridded city, gazing in the windows to the office cubicles and waiting rooms, through the transparent back wall to the next set of cubicles. The camera quietly leads us along, scanning the buildings back and forth, doubling back on itself. What is seen in this city, more often than not, are reflections and tricks of the light, the glass of the city casting illusions of presence: pedestrians passing by appearing as if indoors, office clerks seemingly running around an adjacent building. The camera in *Playtime* is usually on the outside looking in, following from the other side of a glass door, a transparent cubicle partition or a floor-to-ceiling window, as the city's inhabitants go to meetings, go shopping or relax at home.

The sense of how we see ourselves, and see others, in buildings has changed since Stein watched Hamlet and since Tati built his glass microcosm. Stein's 'thing' has morphed; our lives are more visible, more public, more narrated than any other point in human history. The theatre's walls are gone, but its dynamic has diffused. It's here in the networked, glass city – and it could be any city – that Shakespeare's 'all the world's a stage' becomes a truism.

The first time I saw *Playtime*, what struck me most was its wandering camera, how its rambling gaze linked together a city of framed spaces. The camera guides us along the grid, left to right, up, back and over again, as if the building were a page in the act of being read. *Playtime* asks us to reread the surfaces of the city and its boxed-off inhabitants in a specific way – it suggests that these spaces could be read in the same way as reading a page from a comic book.

Imagine a building of apartments: three square rooms next to each other, stacked three stories high. Through each of the nine windows, arranged identically, a low sofa and a chair around a television can be seen. A bouquet of flowers perched on a cabinet is on the other side of the room. A waist-high pot plant with large leaves sits on the floor by the window. Peering into this building, glancing from each square window one room to the next, is to look at several apartments with tiny living rooms that are all done up the same; maybe they were all identically furbished by a lazy landlord, or maybe they even share the same uninspired interior decorator. Looking at the building, what is seen are nine different spaces that are seen at the same time.

Look again, but as a comic-book page.

The page is divided into a grid of three by three. In the top left frame, the sitting room with its sofa, chair, television and cabinet with bouquet can be seen as before. Next, to the right is the same room again, and again to the right, below that six more times filling the rest of the page. However, this time, the room in each square window is no longer a set of adjacent neighbours but now one and the same room. Reading this page, each room-slash-frame becomes a beat in the passage of time; it could be seconds, minutes, hours, years. The relationship to how the building is read is reversed: same space, different time.

Our eyes might, like Tati's camera, dart and stray as they naturally do. Looking from the top-right 'floor' on the page to the bottom left, the sitting room might appear unchanged but our glance suddenly becomes a skip forward missing out on a few moments, or a decade. On the comic page, time is crystallised, choreographed only by the eye; any move to another window frame is a jump in time. Looking in at the details of one frame, like the pot plant by the window, then darting across to look at a room in an identical adjacent building (a facing page) – before doubling back again to step back and take it all in – is a quick, casual jump back and forth in the comic book's chronology. Add people to the mix, as they go about their lives within the building, and the possibilities multiply. It's up to the reader to fill in the narrative blanks when occupants of the comic book's one room are replaced, or disappear.

Architecture, Portman once said breezily, should be a symphony. The symphony he has in mind is apparently crashing, overbearing, drowning out any other sound in the vicinity. Reading Portman's hollowed out atrium as a page, as it unwraps and stretches out around us, lets a quieter, bristling unease emerge. Each hotel room becomes the one room; peering into the hundreds of doorways there are instances of sleeping, listless time wasting, or the interminable cleaning between guests, all occurring at what can be imagined as widely disparate points in time. With each new guest, the building becomes a more compact story of displaced lives – people check in and out, flip through television channels, pace the floor or look out the window, seconds and centuries apart. Dozens and dozens of coexisting time-lines are there to be read, made all the more poignant for taking place in the one small room.

On the city's surfaces might be one way to renegotiate our relationship to time, and to each other. Reading the buildings that hem in the city as a comic-book page provides a means to create inadvertent, unexpected, and at the very least entertaining, narra-tives. As cities continue to expand, finding other ways of looking, ways that seek the disorientation of a new syncopation, are imperative. The building-page is a re-minder of the fact that walls are markers of time and that the past always coexists in the present; it can be used to turn vistas into pan-temporal jumbles, and to suggest pathways that might reconnect and rewire seeing and reading, nervousness and narration. We might then find ourselves reading into the cities' horizons parallel stories that are inexplicably careering, as we look out on new unstable vistas together and trace where we might live, play and learn.

A H - H A

AH
CR
TA

Copy Press is committed to
bringing readers and writers
together and invites you to join
its Reader's Union – please visit
www.copypress.co.uk